Once Upon A Time...

TORMONT

© 1998 Tormont Publications Inc.
338 Saint Antoine Street East
Montreal, Canada
H2Y 1A3
Tel. (514) 954-1441
Fax (514) 954-5086

Illustrations and graphic design: Zapp
Texts by Jane Brierley and Robyn Bryant
Printed in the U.S.A.

CONTENTS

THE
UGLY DUCKLING

IT WAS A golden afternoon in late summer. Near a big old house in the country, a mother duck had made her nest by the water.

"These eggs are taking a long time to hatch!" she sighed. She was lonely sitting there all by herself. The other ducks were too busy swimming around to come and chat with her.

AT LAST the ducklings began to peck their way out of the eggs. Their little beaks banged away against the shell. One by one, still wet from the egg, they tumbled onto the floor of the nest. Soon, they stood up and shook themselves until their soft downy feathers became dry and fluffy.

The little ducklings stared with wonder. "How big the world is!" they chirped, and so it seemed after being inside an egg.

"Oh, the world's much bigger than this," quacked the mother duck. "Now, is everyone hatched? Oh dear, no! That big egg is still there!"

AN OLD DUCK swam by and stopped to look. "That must be a turkey egg," she said. "I had one in my nest once. What a worry it was! The chick wouldn't go near the water however much I tried to push it. Just leave it alone, that's my advice." And she slowly swam away.

"All the same, I'll sit on it a bit longer," the mother duck thought to herself.

Before long, the mother duck heard a tap! tap! and soon the new baby toppled out of the egg. "Chirp! Chirp!" it cried.

The mother stared. "It certainly isn't a turkey," she thought, noticing the webbed feet, "but it's awfully big and ugly. Well, I'll just have to make the best of it."

THE NEXT DAY, the mother duck led her family into the water. Splash! In went the first duckling. One by one they disappeared under the surface and bobbed up again like little balloons. Soon all of them, even the ugly duckling, were gliding over the water.

The mother then took her family to the barnyard. "Bow to the old duck," she said. "The ribbon around her foot means that no one wants to get rid of her, and that's a great honor." The ducklings bowed, too much in awe to even chirp.

Then the turkey marched up to look them over. "I've never seen such a big, ugly duckling!" he gobbled.

THAT WAS the beginning of the duckling's troubles. Everyone was mean to him because he was so ugly. The other ducklings bit him and the hens pecked him. The poor duckling was heartbroken.

As time went by it just got worse. Everyone seemed to hate the poor duckling because he looked different.

One day, the ugly duckling couldn't stand it any longer. He ran out of the barnyard as fast as his big, webbed feet would go. Soon, he was in the woods, and it became harder and harder to find his way. But he kept on running until he could go no further. He found himself beside a great marsh where wild ducks lived. There he lay, hidden under a bush, feeling very lonely and tired.

IN THE MORNING, some wild ducks flew by and stopped to look at the new arrival.

"Hello," they said. "Who are you?"

"I'm a farm duck," said the ugly duckling. He stared at the wild ducks, who looked very different from those in the barnyard.

"A duck?" they squawked. "We've never seen a clumsy little duckling like you! But we don't mind if you stay here a while… the marsh is big enough for all of us."

The ugly duckling was glad to rest by the marsh, far away from the cruel animals on the farm.

THERE WAS a chill in the air. The ugly duckling noticed that the trees were turning gold and red. As he poked among the reeds for food, two young wild geese landed beside him.

"Hi there, friend!" they called. "Would you like some company? We're flying to another marsh a little farther along, where there are lots of young geese like us." And up they flew once more.

The ugly duckling was happy to follow. But before he could move, a shot rang out. To his horror, the geese fell into the marsh, and a huge dog splashed into the water to fetch them.

Guns began firing all around the marsh. Another dog came trotting through the reeds and almost stepped on the ugly duckling. It looked at him for a moment then ran away.

"Thank goodness!" gasped the duckling. "I'm so ugly even the dogs don't want me."

H E LAY perfectly still in the reeds the whole day long. Finally, as the sun began to set, the dogs disappeared and the firing stopped. The duckling scrambled onto the shore and hurried away through the woods.

The wind was blowing very hard as he stumbled along in the dark. Suddenly, he found himself standing in front of a tumbledown old cottage.

A faint light was shining through holes in the door. "I must get out of this wind," thought the duckling. So he squeezed through a hole and huddled in a corner for the night.

An old woman lived in the cottage with her cat and hen.

"And who's this?" she asked the next morning, when she discovered the duckling. "Perhaps you'll give me some ducks eggs, eh?"

The duckling was allowed to stay. The cat and the hen tried to reassure him. "Just lay eggs and learn to purr, and you'll be fine."

BUT THE POOR duckling could do neither of these things, so he sat sadly in the corner, remembering the joy of gliding over the water. At last he said to the hen, "I want to go into the wide world."

"You're crazy," said the hen, "but I won't stop you."

The duckling managed to find a big pond, and there he floated in the sunshine, day after day. Once, a flock of great white birds with long, graceful necks flew by. He had never seen such beautiful birds.

"If only I could be their friend," he thought.

THE COLD winter winds began to blow. The duckling had to paddle hard to keep ice from forming. One morning his feet froze into the ice among the reeds.

A passing farmer saved him. He took the poor bird back to his warm home. But later, the farmer's children frightened the duckling. He flapped about the kitchen, knocking things over, and when the door opened for a moment, out he flew!

Somehow, the duckling survived the winter. One morning, as he lay among the reeds, he noticed how strong the sun felt. He stretched his wings and flew up into the warm air. Before he knew it, he was flying towards a garden with a big pond in the middle.

THERE HE saw three beautiful white birds gliding gracefully over the water. They were swans, but he didn't know it.

"I'll join them," he thought. "Perhaps they'll kill me because I'm so ugly, but I'd rather die that way than be pecked by hens."

He glided over to the swans and bowed his head and there, reflected in the water, was another beautiful swan!

"Look, there's a new one!" cried two little children who had run into the garden. "It's the prettiest one of them all!"

The swan, no longer an ugly duckling, lifted his graceful neck. How delighted he was! His heart filled with love for the other swans, and at last he knew true happiness.

THE
LITTLE TIN
SOLDIER

ONCE UPON a time, a tinsmith made a set of toy soldiers out of some old tin. The soldiers stood very straight, each carrying a gun on his shoulder, and they wore smart red jackets, blue trousers, and tall black hats with gold badges on the front. There wasn't quite enough tin to finish the last soldier, however, so he had only one leg.

The tinsmith then took
the soldiers to a toyshop and very soon they
were bought as a birthday present for a small boy. The one-legged soldier
was the first to be taken out of the box as the boy opened his presents in
front of his brother and sister.

THE SOLDIER found himself facing a paper castle with glass swans floating around it on a little glass lake. But the loveliest toy of all was a little paper ballerina with a pink muslin skirt, standing at the castle door. A big sequin twinkled on her blue sash. The little dancer held her arms above her and lifted her leg behind her so that it was hidden.

"That's the girl for me!" thought the soldier, believing she was one-legged like him.

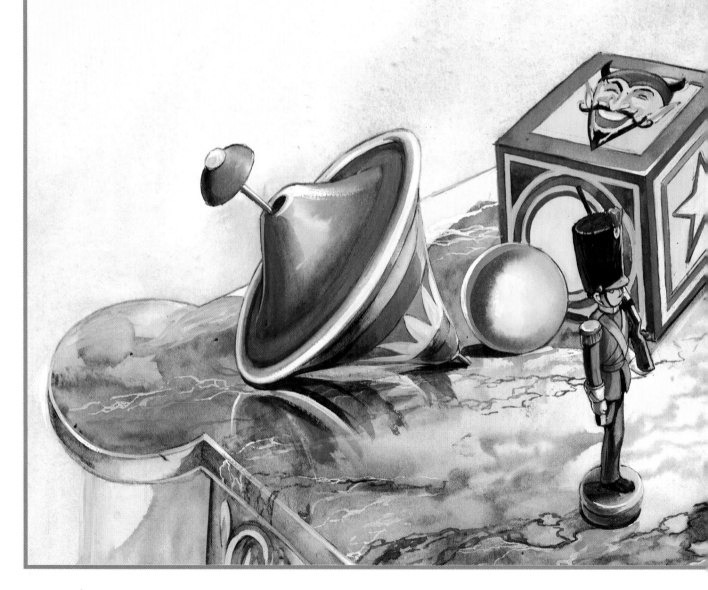

THAT NIGHT, when all the people in the house had gone to bed, the toys began to play. The nutcracker did somersaults while the other toys danced and ran about. The only toys that didn't move were the tin soldier and the lovely paper ballerina. They just stood and gazed at each other.

Suddenly, the clock struck midnight and, with a *snap!*, the jack-in-the-box lid flew back, and a wicked-looking goblin sprang up.

"Keep your eyes to yourself, tin soldier!" he cried. But the soldier just kept staring straight ahead.

"Very well. Just wait until tomorrow!" growled the goblin.

THE NEXT morning, the little boy played with his soldier for a while then put him on the sill by the open window. Perhaps it was the wind, or perhaps it was the goblin, but before he knew it, the soldier was blown out of the window.

The little boy ran to the window and looked out. He stared at the street, three floors below, but couldn't see anything.

"Please, couldn't I go down and look for my soldier?" he asked the maid. But she shook her head. It was raining much too hard for the little boy to go outside.

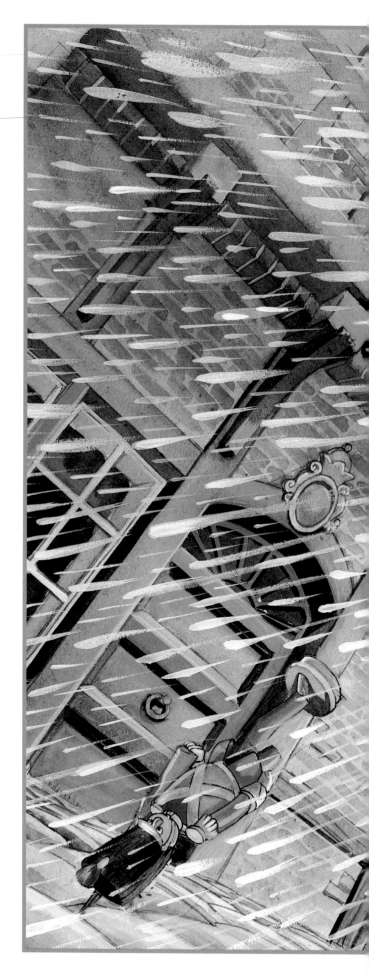

THE MAID shut the window firmly, leaving the little boy looking sadly through the windowpane.

Down below, two street urchins were playing in the rain. They found the tin soldier, wedged upside-down with his gun stuck between two paving stones.

"Let's make him a boat!" they cried, for the street gutter was so full that it had become a real stream. Taking an old newspaper, they folded it into a paper hat, tucked the soldier into the brim, then set the hat afloat in the gutter.

THE SOLDIER stood erect, staring straight ahead as his boat rushed along. The next thing he knew, it had drifted into a long dark drain.

"Where am I going now?" he sighed. "This must be the goblin's fault. If only the beautiful ballerina were here with me, I wouldn't mind."

Just then a huge rat rose up beside the boat. "Stop! Where's your passport?" it screeched.

But the boat rushed on, going faster and faster.

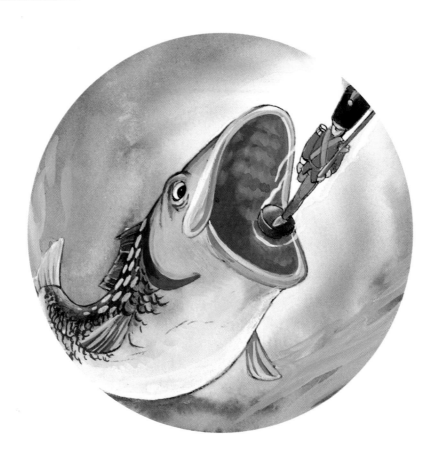

THE PAPER boat tumbled out of the drain and into the canal. By now it was so soggy that it couldn't stay afloat. It began to sink. Finally, it fell apart, and the tin soldier, standing as straight as ever, sank down, down, down... but almost at once a big fish gobbled him up.

"How dark it is in here!" he thought. "Even darker than in my box!"

THE FISH swam down the canal and out to sea, carrying the tin soldier in its stomach. The soldier dreamed of the big room with the children, the toys, the paper castle, and the lovely ballerina.

"I guess I'll never see them again – never see her again," he sighed. He couldn't imagine where he was or what was happening to him. But, as luck would have it, the fish swam into a net and was soon hauled aboard a fishing boat.

THE BOAT brought its catch back to the city, and soon the fish was laid out in the fishmonger's stall. Before long, who should come by but the maid from the little boy's house. She looked at all the different fish, and finally bought the biggest — the one with the soldier inside.

THE MAID went home and delivered the fish to the cook.

"What a fine fish!" exclaimed the cook. She picked up a big knife and started to prepare the fish for the oven. First, she slit open the stomach. "There's something hard in here," she muttered. Then, to her surprise, she pulled out the tin soldier.

The maid recognized it right away. "It's the young master's lost soldier!" she cried.

THE LITTLE boy was very happy when he heard that his lost soldier had been found. As for the tin soldier, he was a little dizzy at first from the bright light, after being so long in the dark. Finally, he realized where he was.

He saw the very same toys on the table, and the pretty paper castle with its glass lake. Right in front of him was the lovely dancer, still standing on one leg. If he'd had any extra tin for tears, he would have wept. Instead, he just gazed at her, and she gazed back.

ALL OF A sudden, the little boy's brother grabbed the tin soldier. "Ugh!" he shouted. "This soldier's no good. He's only got one leg. And besides, he smells like fish!"

Then to everyone's horror, the angry child threw the tin soldier into the fire.

Landing upright, the tin soldier glowed brightly in the flames, but his colors disappeared as he began to melt. Suddenly a puff of wind blew the little dancer off the castle steps, and like a bird she flew into the fire with him. One bright flare… and she was gone.

In the morning, the maid emptied the grate. Among the ashes she found a lump of tin shaped like a heart, and beside it, burnt black as coal, lay the ballerina's sequin.

RUMPELSTILTSKIN

THERE ONCE was a miller who was
very poor. The only thing he had
in the whole wide world was his
beautiful daughter.

One day, the miller was called before the king because he had not paid his taxes. The miller had no money at all, so he told the king,

"I have a daughter who can spin straw into gold."

"Bring her to me," ordered the king.

THAT NIGHT, the king took the miller's daughter to a room filled with straw. "You must spin this straw into gold by morning," he said, "or you and your father will be punished." Then he locked the door.

But the poor girl had no idea
how to spin straw into gold. She
sat down at the spinning-wheel
and did her best to twist the
straw into thread, but it was no
use. She threw herself on the
floor and wept.

SUDDENLY, the door opened and an odd little man walked in.

"Good evening, mistress miller. Why are you crying?" he asked.

"I'm supposed to spin this straw into gold, but I don't know how," she sobbed.

"What will you give me if I spin it for you?" the little man asked.

"I could give you my necklace," said the girl, handing it to him.

"Well, I suppose that will have to do," said the little man and he sat down at the spinning-wheel.

By morning, all the straw had been spun into gold.

WHEN THE king saw the room full of gold, he became even greedier. He took the girl to an even bigger room filled with even more straw, and ordered her to spin it all into gold. The girl could not believe her eyes and ears. "What am I going to do?" she thought to herself.

That night, the little man found the girl crying once again. This time, he agreed to spin the straw into gold in return for her gold ring.

WHEN THE king saw so much gold, he became greedier still. He locked the girl into a huge tower packed to the rafters with straw.

"If you spin this into gold by morning," he said, "I will make you my queen."

That night the little man returned. But the girl had nothing left to give him.

"Then when you marry, you must give me your first child," he said.

The girl could not think of another solution, and agreed.

THE NEXT day, the king found to
his pleasure that the huge room
was filled with gold. As he had
promised, he married the miller's
daughter and she became queen.

A year later, the new queen had a
baby daughter.

THE QUEEN spent the whole night making a long list of all the names she had ever heard.

The next day, she read all the names to the little man, beginning with Abraham. But to each one, he replied, "No, that's not my name." The following day, the queen sent out messengers to look for names all through the town.

THE MESSENGERS came back with some very odd names, like Ribsofbeef and Muttonchop. But to each one, the little man replied, "That's not my name."

By the third day, the queen was desperate. She sent out her messengers again to search the entire kingdom for any names they might have missed.

At nightfall, the last
messenger returned with a strange tale.

"As I was passing through the forest, I saw an odd little man dancing around a fire," he told the queen. "He was singing: The queen will never win this game, for Rumpelstiltskin is my name!"

THAT NIGHT, the queen asked the little man,

"Is your name Alfalfa?"

"No that's not my name," replied the little man.

"Is your name Zebulon?" she asked.

"No, that's not my name," he repeated.

"Could it be Rumpelstiltskin?" asked the queen, at last.

When he heard this, the little man became so angry that his face turned blue! And he stamped his foot so hard that it broke right through the floor.

RUMPELSTITLSKIN disappeared into the hole in the floor and was never seen again.

As for the queen, she lived happily ever after with the king and her lovely daughter.

THE WILD SWANS

ONCE UPON a time, there lived a king who had eleven sons and a daughter named Elise. The children loved each other very much and were very close. They lived in a beautiful castle, but they played and studied just like children from any large, happy family. Sadly, their mother died shortly after the last little prince was born.

As time went on, the king got over the sadness of his wife's death. He met a beautiful woman and fell in love. He asked her to become his queen, not knowing she was really a witch.

"I will have a living companion, and my children will have a mother once more," he thought to himself. But as soon as she set foot in the castle, the new queen hated the children and resolved to get rid of them.

THE QUEEN began telling lies to turn the king against his children. Then, early one morning, she gathered the princes along the castle wall.

"Go!" she ordered. "You shall wander the world with nothing but your wings to help you."

And with a wave of her cloak, she turned them into wild swans – but because they were princes, each had a gold crown on his head.

THE WICKED queen told the king that she had seen the princes running away from the castle. "Let the ungrateful wretches go," she said. Then she sent Elise to live with a peasant family, telling the king that his daughter needed to be with other children.

When Elise turned fifteen, the king decided to send for her. The queen pretended to welcome her kindly. "Come my dear," she said. "You must get ready to meet your father."

WHILE ELISE undressed for her bath, the queen used her magic to summon three huge toads. She picked them up, one by one, and gave each a kiss and a command. "I want you to sit on Elise's head and make her stupid. You shall lie near her heart and harden it, and you shall hop onto her forehead and make her ugly." Then she threw the toads into the bath and soon the water turned a sickly green.

But Elise's innocence and sweetness broke the witch's spell. The toads turned into scarlet poppies, and the water became as clear as crystal.

The queen flew into a rage. She grabbed the girl, rubbed walnut juice on her face, and tied knots in her hair.

When Elise appeared before the king, he was shocked and angry. "This child is not my daughter!" he exclaimed. "Father! It's me Elise!" cried the poor girl. "Ha! A dirty wretch who's after your gold!" snorted the queen.

"Take her away!" the king ordered.

POOR ELISE crept away into the forest, brokenhearted. She missed her brothers more than ever and longed to hear of them. As she sat by a stream, washing her face and untangling her hair, an old woman appeared behind her.

"Have you ever seen eleven princes wandering about?" asked Elise hopefully.

"No, my dear child, but I have seen eleven swans with little gold crowns on their heads," the old woman replied. "They often come to the water's edge at dusk." She pointed through the woods to a large lake.

Elise ran to the shore and waited. At sunset, she heard the beating of wings, and, sure enough, down from the sky came eleven wild swans wearing crowns.

At first, Elise was frightened and hid behind a rock.

ONE BY ONE, the swans swooped down to the shore. As they landed, they shook off their feathers. Watching from her hiding place, Elise was amazed to discover that they were her brothers!

"Anton, Sebastian, it's me, Elise!" she cried, calling out their names as she ran into their arms. The brothers could hardly believe their eyes and ears as they gathered around their long lost sister.

What a happy reunion it was! The brothers told Elise how the wicked witch had cast a spell on them, and she explained how she had been banished from the castle.

"We are swans by day, and become human at sunset," explained Anton, the oldest brother.

"I will find a way to break the spell," Elise assured them.

THE BROTHERS found a large piece of cloth for Elise to lie on. Then, as the sun rose and the princes turned back into swans, they gently lifted her up and flew away. Sebastian, the youngest, dropped berries into her lap for food. By sunset, they had reached a secret cave in a far-off forest.

That night, Elise dreamed of a fairy flying above her on a leaf.

"You can break the spell if you are prepared to suffer," whispered the fairy. "You must collect stinging nettles from a graveyard and knit eleven shirts from their soft flax. When you have finished them all, throw them over your brothers and the spell will be broken. But beware! Until you are finished you must not speak or laugh."

"I don't care!" cried Elise in her dream. "Ill do anything to save my brothers!"

WHEN ELISE woke up it was morning and her brothers had gone. On the floor beside her lay a huge pile of sharp nettles. She set to work at once. By the time the princes returned to the cave, they found Elise knitting a curious garment. Her hands were scratched and her fingers were blistered from making the flax.

"What are you doing?" asked Sebastian. But Elise could say nothing.

Tears rose in Sebastian's eyes as he bent over his sister to watch her work. The tears spilled onto her fingers, and at once the blisters disappeared. She smiled at him gratefully but dared not speak or laugh.

The brothers watched for a while. The whole thing was so mysterious that they began to understand that some kind of magic was at work. Perhaps Elise was trying to save them.

EARLY THE next morning, after the brothers had flown away, Elise stepped outside the cave. "I'll take my work and sit in that leafy oak," she thought. "No one will see me there."

Before long, however, a group of hunters spotted her. "Who are you, girl?" they shouted roughly. When she didn't respond, they dragged her down from the tree.

"Stop!" cried a voice, and a young king came riding up.

"What is your name?" asked the young king, kindly. Elise just shook her head and smiled. "She shall come with me," said the king, dismissing the hunters.

They returned to his castle. The king tried speaking to Elise in several different languages, all the while watching her knit. Although she said nothing, her gentle glance and lovely face captured the king's heart.

ELISE NOW lived in luxury, but still she spent most of her time knitting quietly. The king often sat with her, and found happiness in her company. At last he spoke to the archbishop. "I love this sweet maiden and I mean to marry her," he announced.

The archbishop was horrified. "You know nothing about the girl! She could be a witch for all we know. What about her strange knitting?"

But the king was determined. He spoke to Elise, who clasped his hand lovingly, but still kept silent. They were married soon after.

Elise continued knitting until she had no more nettles left. That night, she went to pick nettles from a graveyard. A group of witches had gathered there, but Elise cared only about her brother's shirts.

Meanwhile, the archbishop ran to get the king. "Your wife is up to no good!" he warned.

The king followed him, and to his horror found Elise crouching on the ground, while three hideous witches cackled over a nearby grave.

"I can't believe it!" cried the brokenhearted king. "Do what you must."

ELISE was accused of witch-craft.

"Wife, say you are innocent, I beg you," pleaded the king. But Elise could only gaze at him sadly.

The next morning, she was taken to the market square to be burnt at the stake. She was still knitting, and beside her lay a pile of ten shirts. As the cart passed through the crowd, the angry mob shouted "Burn the witch!"

Suddenly, the sky grew dark as eleven swans swooped down beside her. Quickly, she threw the shirts over them. The crowd gasped as the great swans turned into princes.

Sebastian, who got the eleventh shirt with only one sleeve, still had one wing.
"Save me!" Elise cried out at last. "I am innocent!"

ELISE, surrounded by her brothers, went up to the king. Tears of joy fell from her eyes as she told the story of the spell cast by her wicked stepmother, how she had found her brothers and why she kept silent while knitting the nettle shirts.

The king also wept for joy and clasped his wife tenderly. "My darling, only someone with your goodness of heart would make such a sacrifice."

The crowd cheered "God bless the queen!" Then Elise noticed Sebastian's wing. "Oh, your poor arm!" she cried in distress.

"Don't be sad," he said, hugging her. "I will carry my swan's wing proudly, as the symbol of a sister's unselfish love."

LITTLE RED
RIDING HOOD

ONCE UPON a time, there was a little girl who lived on the edge of the forest. Whenever she went out, she wore the lovely red riding cloak that her grandmother had given her, so everyone called her Little Red Riding Hood.

One morning, a messenger brought a letter. "Oh dear, said Little Red Riding Hood's mother. "Your grandmother is not feeling well."

"Homemade soup might make her feel better," the little girl suggested.

"That's a good idea," her mother said. So they packed a nice basket for Little Red Riding Hood to take to her grandmother.

WHEN THE BASKET of food was ready, the little girl put on her red cloak and kissed her mother goodbye.

"Remember, go straight to Granny's house," said her mother. "Don't wander off the path! The woods are dangerous."

"Don't worry mother," said Little Red Riding Hood. "I won't."

BUT WHEN Little Red Riding Hood noticed some flowers in the woods, she quickly forgot her promise. She picked a few here, and a few there, and soon she had strayed quite far from the path.

Suddenly, a great big wolf appeared beside her.

"Who are you and what are you doing here little girl?" snarled the wolf.

"THEY CALL ME Little Red Riding Hood," she replied, "and I'm on my way to see my Granny, who is not feeling well."

"You had better let me take you back to the path then," the wolf said. "There is a wolf in the neighborhood, you know."

"What does a wolf look like?" asked Little Red Riding Hood.

"Oh, they have very long purple ears," said the wolf. "And where does your dear Granny live?" he asked.

Little Red Riding Hood told him precisely, for she was a polite girl, even if she was not very obedient. Then she continued on the path to Granny's house. The wolf, in the meantime, took a shortcut.

THE CLEVER wolf sped through the woods all the way to Granny's house. In no time at all, he was standing at her door. He paused for a moment to catch his breath, then he knocked ever so gently.

"Who is it?" Granny called from her bed.

"It's Little Red Riding Hood," the wolf replied in a high sweet voice.

"Oh, how lovely! Do come in, my dear," said Granny.

So the wolf let himself in. Poor Granny did not have time to say another word before the wolf gobbled her up.

THE WOLF let out a satisfied burp, and then poked through Granny's wardrobe to find a nightgown that he liked. He added a frilly sleeping cap, and dabbed some of Granny's perfume behind his pointy ears.

When he was all dressed, he posed in front of the mirror, and practised Granny's voice. "Oh, how lovely! Do come in!" he croaked, until he was satisfied.

A FEW MINUTES later, Little Red Riding Hood knocked on the door. The wolf jumped into bed and pulled the covers over his nose.

"Who is it?" he called in a cackly voice.

"It's me, Little Red Riding Hood."

"Oh, how lovely! Do come in, my dear," squeaked the wolf.

Little Red Riding Hood put her basket on the kitchen table, and gave her grandmother a kiss on the cheek.

"Poor Granny," she said. "You don't look like yourself at all! I'm going to make you a nice hot lunch."

"That sounds lovely," said the wolf.

"YOUR VOICE sounds loud and scratchy," said Little Red Riding Hood as she sliced some bread.

"Oh, well. The better to greet you with, my dear," said the wolf.

"THIS SOUP might help," said Little Red Riding Hood. "We made your favorite, chicken."

"Thank you, dear," said the wolf.

Then the little girl noticed the lumps in Granny's cap.

"Are your ears bothering you Granny? They are so big!"

"They are a bit swollen. But the better to hear you with, my dear," said the wolf.

But as he spoke, the nightgown slipped down from over his nose.

"Oh my!" said Little Red Riding Hood. "What big teeth you have!"

"The better to eat you with, my dear!" growled the wolf.

IN A FLASH, Little Red Riding Hood had joined her granny in the wolf's belly.

The wolf burped again and lay down for a little nap. But he was snoring so loud that he drew the attention of a passing hunter.

"Something seems to be the matter with Little Red Riding Hood's grandmother," the hunter thought to himself.

The hunter knocked on the door but the wolf was sleeping so soundly that he did not wake up.

The hunter then pushed open the window. As soon as he saw the wolf asleep in the bed in Granny's clothes, he understood exactly what had happened.

He quickly took aim and fired his musket, killing the wolf in one shot.

"Take that you nasty creature!" he cried.

THE HUNTER wanted to make sure the wolf was dead, so he listened for a heartbeat. Instead, he heard faint voices crying for help. He carefully cut the wolf's belly open. Out stepped Little Red Riding Hood and her Granny, safe and sound.

"Oh, Granny, I was so scared!" said the girl. "I promise I will not wander off the path again!"

The grandmother thanked the hunter and the three of them sat down together to eat the nice lunch that Little Red Riding Hood had brought.

A little later, the hunter escorted Little Red Riding Hood back to her house.

"Oh there you are," said her mother. "How is Granny feeling?"

"Much better now," said Little Red Riding Hood.

THE BRAVE LITTLE TAILOR

ONCE UPON a time, a little tailor was sitting at his workbench sewing, when he heard a woman's voice in the street below.

"Jam for sale," called the woman.

Sticking his head out the window, the tailor beckoned to the woman.

"Up here, my good woman," he shouted. "I'll buy your jam."

THE WOMAN carried her heavy basket all the way up three flights of stairs to the tailor's room, and laid out all the jams and jellies.

The tailor opened every single jar and sniffed each kind. Finally he said, "I'll buy three spoonfuls of this one."

The woman was disappointed to sell such a small amount, but she measured it out and went on her way.

THE TAILOR spread the jam on some bread, and put it down beside him. "I'll eat it as soon as I finish this shirt," he said to himself.

The smell of the jam soon attracted a number of flies.

"Get out of here," the tailor yelled. But the flies didn't understand his language and kept buzzing around the jam.

Finally the angry tailor struck at them with a piece of cloth. Seven flies fell to the ground, dead.

"SEVEN! That's amazing!" said the little tailor. "The whole world should know about this!"

So he made himself a leather belt, and on it wrote SEVEN WITH ONE BLOW.

Then he put on his new belt and headed out into the world.

On the way out, he grabbed an
old piece of cheese, and stuck
it in his pocket in case he got
hungry.

Just outside the door, he found
a bird, and for no special reason
he stuck that in his pocket, too.

OUTSIDE of town, he came across a terrible looking giant. "Hello there," said the tailor. "I am going to seek my fortune in the wide world. Would you care to join me?"

The giant just laughed. "Don't be silly, you little crumb!"

The tailor was annoyed. "Look at my belt if you want to see what kind of man I am!" he said.

WHEN THE giant read the words on the belt, he thought the tailor had killed seven men. Still, he couldn't quite believe that such a small man could be so strong, so he decided to test him.

The giant picked up a rock and squeezed it until water came out.

"I bet you can't do that," he said.

The tailor took the old cheese out of his pocket and squeezed it until whey came out.

THE GIANT was not convinced. So he threw the rock far into the distance.

"Try that," he said.

"Not bad," said the tailor. "But I notice it fell back down to earth."

Then the tailor pulled the bird from his pocket and threw it in the air. The bird, pleased to be free, flew out of sight.

"WELL, IF you're so strong, help me carry this tree," the giant said, pointing to a huge oak.

"Certainly," said the tailor. "You take the trunk and I'll carry the fat end, which is no doubt much heavier."

The giant, walking in front, could not see the tailor riding in the branches.

THE TAILOR was truly enjoying the ride and soon fell asleep cradled in the branches. But after a while, the giant woke him up. "I'm tired," he said. "I have to put it down for a minute."

The tailor quickly jumped down and grabbed the branches to make it look as if he had been carrying the tree all along. "I guess you're not as strong as you thought," he said to the giant.

T HEY WALKED on until they came to a cherry tree covered with fruit. The best cherries were at the top, so the giant bent the tree over for the tailor to pick some.

But when the little tailor grabbed hold of the top branch, the tree straightened up, flinging him right over the top.

"You can't even hold down a little branch!" said the giant.

"Of course I can," replied the tailor. "I jumped over the tree on purpose. See if you can."

THE GIANT tried to jump over but got his foot caught in the branches. Just then the king and his attendants came riding by. "What's this?" the king asked.

"Why nothing much, Your Highness. I've just captured this giant," said the tailor.

Since the giant had been a great nuisance in the neighborhood, the king rewarded the tailor with a bag of gold.

SOON, everyone in the land had heard about the brave little tailor who captured the giant.

And so the little tailor found fame and fortune and lived happily
ever after.

THE EMPEROR'S NEW CLOTHES

THERE WAS once a very
grand emperor who loved
fine clothes. He spent almost
all his time and a great deal of
money on splendid new outfits.

THE EMPEROR wasn't very interested in governing the country, and only appeared in public to show off some new fashion.

One day, two swindlers arrived in the emperor's city and decided they would take advantage of his fondness for clothes.

"I have a plan," said one to the other, "that will make us rich in no time!"

THE PALACE guards had orders to admit all weavers and tailors, and the two strangers were soon talking to the emperor.

"We are weavers from a faraway country, where the most wonderful clothes in the world are worn. Our cloth has unbelievably beautiful colors and patterns," they told the emperor, who listened eagerly.

"This very fine cloth," they added slyly, "is invisible to anyone who is stupid or unsuited for his post."

"How useful that would be!" the emperor said to himself. "I'd be able to tell the wise from the foolish, and find out who isn't fit for his post."

He then ordered his prime minister to give the men money, as well as sacks of silk and gold thread so that they could get started.

THE TWO swindlers lost no time. They rented a big workshop and a loom, and settled in comfortably. Whenever anyone came by, they pretended to be hard at work.

Of course, they weren't really weaving at all. They hid a bit of the precious silk and gold thread each day, and spent their time eating and drinking.

MEANWHILE, the emperor thought about how wonderful his new clothes were going to be.

"I wonder how those weavers are coming along with their work," he thought to himself. He was a little hesitant about going to see for himself, since the cloth had such magical qualities… not that he need worry!

"I know! I'll send my prime minister!" exclaimed the emperor. "He's not stupid, and he's certainly fit for his post, so the cloth won't be invisible to him."

The emperor summoned the prime minister and told him to bring a detailed report of the new cloth.

THE NEWS about the weavers who were making the wonderful new cloth had spread throughout the city. The prime minister, who was indeed a wise man, decided it would be best to visit the weavers alone.

"Of course, I know I'm fit for my post, and not stupid, but it's best to be on the safe side."

When he arrived, the swindlers were ready for him. Waving their arms grandly, they described the beautiful colors and patterns. One held up cloth that was finished; the other showed him the cloth still on the loom. But the poor prime minister couldn't see a thing!

"Is it possible I am really stupid?" he thought.

THE PRIME minister returned to the emperor.

"Your majesty," he said solemnly, "I have never seen anything like it." Then he paused, at a loss for words.

"Well? What is it like?" asked the impatient emperor.

"Ah, your majesty… the colors are exquisite, like a beautiful sunset — blue, mauve, pink, and gold. And such intricate patterns — like a garden, with delicate flowers, graceful trees, and rushing streams. I can't believe how clever these weavers are!"

AFTER A while, the swindlers asked the prime minister for more money. The old man felt that something was wrong, but he was afraid to say that he couldn't see the cloth. He agreed to send them money and more thread.

The next day, the emperor's servants arrived at the workshop, bearing more sacks of gold and silk thread, as well as a chest filled with gold coins. The swindlers were delighted.

Soon the emperor grew impatient once more. This time he sent his most fashionable gentleman-in-waiting to see how the weavers were getting along.

The gentleman-in-waiting was shocked to see an empty loom. "Can I be stupid?" he thought. He lifted his eye-glass and pretended to study the cloth.

The gentleman-in-waiting returned to the palace. How could he tell the truth and reveal his stupidity?

And so he, too, praised the beauties of the cloth and described all the wonderful details to the emperor.

AT LAST, the emperor decided to see the cloth for himself. The swindlers bowed low as they showed him the cloth and described its wonders.

The emperor couldn't believe his eyes. The cloth was invisible to him!

"Here, feel this, your majesty!" said one of the swindlers. "This cloth is as light as a feather."

"Hmm… er… yes, yes — very light. Magnificent stuff, absolutely magnificent," said the emperor.

SOON, the weavers arrived at the palace for a fitting. The emperor stood patiently in his underwear while they pretended to measure and fit the cloth. The courtiers oohed and aahed. "Marvellous!" said one. "Incredible!" cried another. "Your majesty, you must show the people your new clothes in the procession tomorrow!"

The next day, the swindlers helped the emperor dress. Carefully, they handed him his new clothes, and, just as carefully, he did his best to put them on.

"Is everything straight?" he asked, looking anxiously at himself in the mirror.

"Oh, yes, your majesty," they exclaimed, grinning from ear to ear.

THE EMPEROR paraded through the city. All the people cheered and exclaimed how fine the new clothes were, because they were afraid to be thought stupid. Suddenly, a little child cried out, "But he's not wearing any clothes!" Soon, everyone was laughing and saying loudly, "The emperor isn't wearing any clothes!"

The emperor heard them and felt deeply ashamed. "They're right,"
he thought. Still, he held his head higher than ever, resolving never to
mention his true stupidity to anyone. As for the clever swindlers, they
disappeared without a trace, taking with them a fortune in gold and fine
thread.

THE FROG PRINCE

ONCE UPON a time, there lived a princess who adored objects made of gold. Her favorite toy in the world was a golden ball.

On hot days, she liked to sit beside an old well in the cool forest, tossing the ball in the air.

One day, the ball slipped from her fingers into the well, which was so deep that the princess could not see the bottom.

"Oh dear! I'll never find it!" the princess said, and she began to cry.

SUDDENLY, a voice called out from below.

"What's the matter, beautiful princess? Why are you crying?"

The princess looked all around but couldn't see anyone.

"Down here, " said the little voice.

The princess looked down and saw a green frog poking its head out of the water.

"Oh, it's only you," she said. "If you must know, I'm upset because my golden ball fell into the well."

"I could get it back for you," said the frog.

"But what will you give me as a reward?"

"WHATEVER you like, frog. How about my pearls and jewels," the princess suggested. "Or perhaps my golden crown?"

"What would I do with a crown?" said the frog.

"But I'll get your ball if you promise I can be your best friend, and come for dinner and sleep over at your house."

"ALL RIGHT. You can be my best friend," said the princess. But secretly she thought the frog was talking a whole lot of nonsense.

The frog dove deep into the well and soon returned with the golden ball in its mouth.

As soon as the frog dropped the ball at the princess's feet, she grabbed it and ran home, without even a thank you.

"Wait!" called the frog. "I can't run that fast."

But the princess paid no attention to him.

T HE PRINCESS forgot all about the frog, but the next day, as she was eating dinner with her family, she heard something come crawling *splish-splash* up the marble steps of the castle.

Then a voice called,

"Princess, open the door!"

The curious princess ran to open it, but when she saw the frog standing there, all green and dripping, she slammed the door in his face.

THE KING could tell that something was the matter.

"Has a giant come to get you?" he asked.

"Oh, no, father. It's only an ugly frog," she replied.

"And what does a frog want with you?" asked the king.

As the princess explained, they heard more knocking.

"Let me in, Princess," the frog pleaded.

"Have you forgotten what you promised down by the well?"

"IF YOU MADE a promise, daughter, you must keep it. Let him in," said the king.

With a long face, the princess opened the door. The frog followed her to the table and said,

" Lift me up beside you."

"Don't be ridiculous," the princess said, but her father gave her such a look that she changed her mind.

The chair wasn't high enough so the frog asked to be lifted onto the table. And once there, he said,

"Push your plate closer so I can share your dinner."

THE PRINCESS moved her plate, but it was quite clear she didn't enjoy the rest of her meal.

Once the frog had eaten his fill, he said,

"I'm tired. Carry me upstairs so I can sleep in your room."

The thought of sharing her room with the cold damp frog so upset the princess that she began to cry again. But the king said,

"Be on your way. It's not right to turn your back on someone who helped you when you were in trouble."

"YES, FATHER," said the princess, and she carefully picked up the frog with two fingers. When she got to her room, she set the frog down in the corner farthest from her bed.

But soon she heard the frog plop down beside her.

"I'm tired, too," said the frog. "Lift me into bed, or I'll tell your father."

SO THE PRINCESS tucked the frog into bed, with his little green head resting on a fluffy pillow.

But when she got back into her bed, she was surprised to hear the frog sobbing quietly.

"What's the matter now, little frog?" she asked.

"All I ever wanted was a friend," the frog replied. "But it's clear you don't like me at all! I might as well go back to the well."

At this, the princess felt very badly indeed.

S HE SAT DOWN on the edge of the frog's bed.
"I'll be your friend," she said, and this time she
meant it.

Then the princess gave him a kiss goodnight on his small
green cheek.

Instantly, the frog was transformed into a very handsome young prince! The princess could not have been more surprised or pleased.

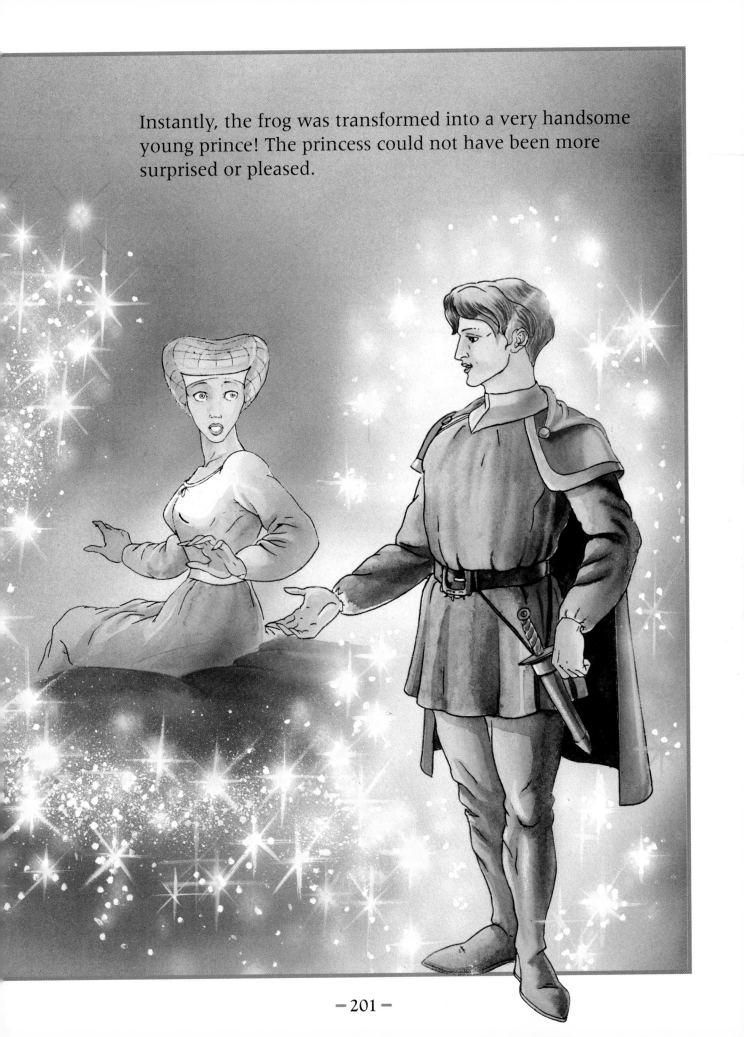

OF COURSE the prince and princess became very good friends indeed. A few years later, they were married and lived happily ever after.

RAPUNZEL

THERE ONCE lived a couple who longed to have a child. Finally, their wish came true.

As the wife waited for the child to be born, she sometimes stared out the window at the garden next door. In it grew some delicious-looking rapunzel lettuce.

But the garden belonged to a witch, and no one dared to go into it.

SOON, the wife could think of nothing but that lettuce. She grew paler and paler. Finally, her worried husband decided to sneak into the garden after dark and pick some.

His wife ate it all, but it only made her want more. So the husband went back to the garden.

BUT THIS time, the witch caught him.

"How dare you steal my rapunzel!" she screeched.

The terrified husband told her of his wife's craving.

"Take all the lettuce you want, then," said the witch. "But in return, you must give me the child."

The poor man agreed.

As soon as the child was born, the witch took it away to raise as her own. She called the baby girl Rapunzel.

Rapunzel grew to be so
beautiful that the witch
decided no one else must
ever see her.

So when the child reached the age of twelve, the witch shut her in a tower deep in the forest. The tower was very tall, and had no door. Poor Rapunzel had no way of escaping.

When the witch came to visit, she called, "Rapunzel, Rapunzel, let down your hair."

Then the girl threw her long braid out the window, and the witch climbed it to the top of the tower.

A FEW YEARS later, a prince happened to be riding through the forest. From a distance he heard Rapunzel singing to amuse herself. He was immediately drawn to the beautiful voice, but once he found the tower, he could find no way in.

THE PRINCE could not stop thinking about the voice in the tower. Every day he would go back to listen and every night he would leave brokenhearted. He still could find no way in.

Until one day from his hiding place, he saw the witch and heard her call.

"Rapunzel, Rapunzel, let down your hair." Then a long braid fell from the window all the way down to the ground.

"If that's the rope to climb, I'll try it," the young prince thought to himself.

AS SOON AS the witch had gone, the prince repeated her call.

"Rapunzel, Rapunzel, let down your hair."

Then he climbed the long braid to the top.

At first Rapunzel was frightened, as she had never before seen a man. But the prince told her how he had been drawn to her sweet voice and asked her to marry him. Rapunzel liked him better than the witch and agreed.

But she still had no way to leave the tower. The prince promised to bring a ball of silk each time he came to visit so she could weave a ladder and escape.

THE PRINCE visited every night, and Rapunzel kept his visits a secret. But one day, without thinking, she blurted out to the witch, "Why are you so much heavier than the prince?"

"How dare you trick me!" screamed the witch, and in a fury, she cut off Rapunzel's long hair.

The witch laid an evil spell on Rapunzel that sent her to a far-off land.
Then she tied the long braid to the windowsill and waited for the prince.
Only as he climbed through the window did he realize he had been tricked.

"Your little songbird is gone," cackled the witch, "and you will never see her
again!"

THE PRINCE was beside himself with grief and leapt from the tower window. He survived the fall by landing in a thornbush, but the thorns scratched his eyes. The prince was blinded! How would he ever find Rapunzel now?

FOR MONTHS to come, the prince wandered blindly through the forest, weeping. Whenever he met people along the way, he would ask if they had seen a beautiful girl named Rapunzel, and he would describe her to them. But no one had ever seen her.

Then one day, the prince heard someone singing a sad but beautiful song. He recognized the voice at once and ran towards it, calling out Rapunzel's name.

RAPUNZEL rushed into the prince's arms and cried tears of joy at finding her beloved. But as her tears fell on the prince's eyes, a strange thing happened – the prince could see again!

Rapunzel and the prince found their way back to the kingdom.
Soon they were married and lived happily ever after.

PUSS 'N BOOTS

THERE WAS once an old miller who had three sons. When he died, he left them everything he had. Simon, the eldest son, inherited the flour mill, Alex got a donkey and Jack, the youngest, got a cat.

SIMON SOON set to work grinding flour. Alex headed for town with his donkey. "I'm going to find work hauling things," he said.

Jack, meanwhile, tried to think of a way to make a living.

"That silly cat is worse than useless, for I shall have to feed him, as well as myself," he grumbled.

"Do not be so glum, Master," the cat said. "I have a plan that will make us both rich."

"WHAT CAN you do? You're only a cat!" said Jack.
"Give me a fine hat, a pair of good boots, and a large sack," said the cat. "I shall take care of the rest."

"Why not," Jack said miserably. "What have I got to lose?"

When the cat was dressed to his satisfaction, he left Jack sitting in a field, and headed for the nearest stream. Puss 'n Boots, as he was then called, crouched on the bank and used his swift paws to pull a dozen gleaming fish out of the water.

HIS SACK bulging with fish, Puss 'n Boots strutted to the castle and asked to see the King.

"What business does a cat have with the King?" asked the gatekeeper.

"I have a gift from the Marquis of Carabas," said Puss. He was allowed in at once, and bowed before the King, the Queen and their daughter, Cecile.

"The Marquis of Carabas sends his greetings, and would like you to have these fine fish from his estate, Your Highness," said the cat.

"Tell the Marquis we appreciate his kindness," said the King. But as soon as Puss had left, the King whispered to his wife, "Who is this Marquis?"

"I don't know," replied the Queen. "I've never even heard of him."

OVER THE NEXT few days, Puss returned to the court several times, each time with a gift for the royal family.

"Here comes that cat again! Who is this Marquis of Carabas?" the courtiers whispered.

Since no one knew who he was, everyone in the King's court made up stories about him.

"I hear he is the richest man in the kingdom," someone said.

"And the most handsome," said another.

THEN ONE DAY, when Puss brought the Queen a pheasant, she said to him, "Your master seems to be a good hunter."

"Oh yes," Puss replied. "The Marquis has many talents."

"But why have we never met him?" asked the Queen. "You must arrange a meeting."

That night, Puss told Jack he was to meet the Queen. "That's ridiculous!" said Jack. "Look at me! I don't even have a decent shirt!"

"Don't you worry," said Puss. "Leave everything to me."

THE NEXT DAY, Puss led Jack to the river.

"Take off your shirt and get in the water," Puss told him.

"But I can't swim!" said Jack.

"Don't worry. Just do as I say," said the cat.

But when Jack stepped into the river, the cat pushed him into deep water. Just as Puss had planned, the current carried Jack downstream to the bridge where the king's carriage was passing.

"Help!" cried Jack.

"Hurry!" yelled Puss. "The Marquis of Carabas is drowning!"

THE KING ordered two men to pull Jack out of the water. He sent a third man to the castle for dry clothing. Soon, Jack was dressed in clothes fit for a marquis.

"He would make a handsome husband, don't you think?" whispered the Queen to Cecile.

"You must be exhausted from your ordeal," the King said to Jack. "We shall escort you home."

"Yes. Where exactly is your castle?" asked the King's advisor, who was suspicious of Jack and his cat.

"Well, ahhh, I don't have a castle," muttered Jack.

"The Marquis is always so modest. There it is," said Puss, pointing to a castle on the hill. "Now, if you will excuse me, I have some errands to run." And the cat leapt out of the carriage.

Puss 'n Boots raced along the road, ahead of the King's carriage, and shouted to the peasants working in the fields.

"If anyone asks, say these lands belong to the Marquis of Carabas," Puss instructed them. "The castle, too."

"Certainly, Sire," the peasants replied.

Puss reached the castle on the hill, and knocked at the huge gate. A door in the gate swung silently open.

Puss tiptoed through the dark rooms. Suddenly, a giant ogre appeared before him.

"What are you doing in my castle?" he hollered.

Puss introduced himself politely.

"I hear you have great magical powers and that you can transform yourself into an elephant, or even a lion," said Puss. "Is that true?"

Instantly, the ogre transformed himself into a lion.

"What do you think?" he roared, chasing Puss around the room.

"I believe you!" said Puss. "But can you make yourself as small as a mouse?"

"I CAN DO anything," replied the proud ogre. But as soon as he transformed himself into a mouse, the clever cat swooped him up and swallowed him whole.

Meanwhile, the King's carriage approached the castle.

"Who owns all these rich fields?" he asked.

"The Marquis of Carabas," replied one of the peasants.

"And the castle is his, too?" asked the King.

"Yes, Sire," said the peasant.

WITH THE OGRE out of the way, Puss ran through the castle, opening all the gloomy curtains to let the sun in. He reached the gate just as the King's carriage pulled up.

"Welcome to the estate of the Marquis of Carabas," Puss announced, bowing low.

"Why it's lovely," said the Queen.

"You've done very well for yourself, young man," said the King.

"Yes, it seems that I have," replied Jack.

But Jack was not looking at the castle at all – from the moment he met her, Jack only had eyes for Princess Cecile.

Several months later, Jack and Cecile were married, and they lived happily ever after. Of course, Puss 'n Boots lived happily ever after at their side.